A
Little
Bigalow
Story

Written and Illustrated by
Barbara Alexander

Oak Tree Publications, Inc.
San Diego, California

A LITTLE BIGALOW STORY is part of the Make Believe & Me series.

A LITTLE BIGALOW STORY text copyright © 1985 by Discovery, Inc. Illustrations copyright © 1985 by Barbara Alexander.

First Edition.

Manufactured in the United States of America.

Creative supervisor and world-wide licensing through Howard Wexler, 300 East 40th Street, New York, New York 10016.

Library of Congress Cataloging-in-Publication Data

Alexander, Barbara, 1940–
  A little Bigalow story.

  (Make believe & me)
  Summary: Bigalow, a pantry mouse, begins a new life as he takes a ride on a helium-filled balloon.
  [1. Mice–Fiction. 2. Balloon ascensions–Fiction] I. Title. II. Series.
PZ7.A3766Li   1985   [E]   85-21391

ISBN   0-86679-021-7

1 2 3 4 5 6 7 8 9 88 87 86 85

For special little boy persons like:
Mikie "Crusher," Mikie G., Josh, "Baby" Charles,
Brian, Daniel and T.J. Alexander

Granny Rose's old house looked like a birthday cake. The outside was all gleamy and icing-white, with flowers growing everywhere.

The inside was always filled with the sweet smells of Granny's cooking.

One day, Katie and T.J. were up before sunrise.

"I was awake all night thinking about the picnic at the lake today," Katie said, hopping on her right foot while looking for her left shoe.

"Gran says we can go fishing and ride in a real boat with oars!" said T.J. He ran a brush through his hair and put on his cap.

From the bottom of the stairs Granny Rose called, "Come to breakfast, children. We have a very long drive ahead of us!" Gran had been up for hours, fixing a picnic of fried chicken, creamy potato salad, fudge brownies, and icy lemonade.

T.J. and Katie hurried through breakfast, gathered up their bathing suits and towels, and helped Granny carry the heavy picnic basket to her little old car.

The sun was just peeking over the trees when Granny said, "Climb in, darlings! We must be on our way if we're to have a full 'lake' day and be back here before dark."

On the third try, Gran's old car finally coughed. On the fourth try, it sputtered into a steady chug and slowly bumped onto the highway.

"Everybody settle down now," Granny said. "It's a long ride to the lake."

"And slow!" T.J. groaned and flopped against the seat.

Just then, Katie noticed something out the rear window. "T.J., look! We're being followed!" She pointed to a tiny trail of billowing dust that seemed to be chasing their car.

"It looks like a little bitty train trying to catch up with us!" T.J. shouted.

"Look now!" squealed Katie. "It's trying to get closer
. . . . I know what it is! It's—it's little Bigalow, the mouse
that lives in Granny's pantry. He wants to come with us to
the lake."

T.J. looked at Katie and blinked. Then he smiled a big
smile. "You *are* make-believing, aren't you, Katie?"

Katie nodded. "Oh, T.J., let's make-believe together
about Bigalow!"

Make-believing was something Katie and T.J. did on
certain special days, and today felt like one of those
days . . . .

Bigalow collapsed into the dust, panting for breath. Granny's car got smaller and smaller in the distance, until soon it was gone from sight.

"Oh, I wanted to go!" the little mouse sobbed into the dirt. "They talk of such wonderful places, and I've never been anywhere."

Bigalow picked himself up and slowly walked back to Granny's house. By the time he had scrambled through the hole in the kitchen screen, he was feeling a little better.

At least, I have the house all to myself today, he thought as he hopped down from the windowsill.

He scurried under the kitchen table looking for tidbits and crumbs. By Katie's chair, he munched on a delicious crust of raisin toast. After that, he ate the chocolate-covered doughnut crumbles that had fallen from T.J.'s napkin. Most mornings, the hungry little mouse watched from his hiding place while Mudpie, the dog, or Cassandra and her kittens gobbled up any scraps that fell. But this quiet morning, Bigalow ate until he was full.

After he had carefully cleaned his whiskers, Bigalow was ready to look around. Although he had lived there quite a while, he hadn't seen much of Granny's house.

Not since the time he had run across the kitchen floor while Gran and Katie were baking cookies and *horrible* things had happened. Katie had shouted *very* loudly and jumped up and down, startling Granny Rose. Granny had thrown up her arms, and a whole plate of hot cookies flew into the air. With that, Cassandra had raced after him. Breathlessly, he had dashed under the corner of the potato box, just ahead of her sharp teeth and claws. Bigalow remembered how his tiny heart had thumped wildly for hours afterward. From then on, he left his little place only at night and never for very long.

So now, alone in the house, Bigalow inspected the kitchen first. He sniffed into all the cupboards. Over cups, glasses, and dishes, he crawled. Up the pots and down the pans, he wandered. From the sugar bowl, he climbed into the flour sack. A second later, he *ah-chooed* himself out again and set off for the parlor, leaving a trail of tiny white footprints.

For hours, Bigalow explored. He looked in every
closet. He peeked into every drawer *and* snooped under
every bed and chair.

By the time he found T.J.'s room, Bigalow was very
tired. With a yawn, the little mouse curled himself into a
forgotten sock under T.J.'s bed and fell fast asleep.

It was afternoon when Bigalow awoke. He remembered the picnic again, and felt too sad to explore anymore. When he crawled out from under the bed to go back to his little place, he looked up and saw it for the first time—a big red balloon floating gracefully above the end of T.J.'s bed. It was truly the most beautiful thing he had ever seen!

How does it stay in the air like that? he thought.

Cautiously, Bigalow crept closer to the bed. Slowly, he climbed the bedpost. Every few steps he stopped and listened for "coming home" sounds from downstairs. When he reached the knotted string, he stepped onto it . . . v-e-r-y carefully. The beautiful balloon held strong and steady without even the slightest wobble.

At that moment, Bigalow got the most fantastical idea a mouse ever had!

This wonderful balloon can take me into the Great, Wide
Outsideness . . . where I can have an adventure like T.J. and
Katie's picnic at the lake! thought Bigalow.
In his excitement, he lost his balance and fell.
THUMP . . . *squeak!*
He rubbed a painful lump on his little head.

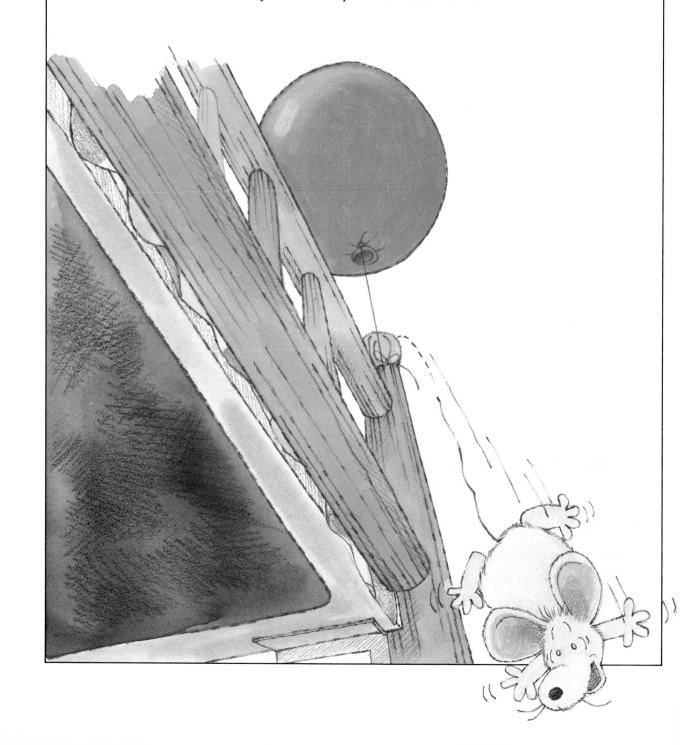

When the hurt stopped, Bigalow scampered
downstairs to the parlor. In Granny's sewing basket, he
found all the heavy thread he thought he would need.

Then he scurried to the trash basket in the pantry. He had burrowed almost to the bottom before he came upon something he could use. Granny Rose had added walnuts when she'd made fudge brownies for the picnic. The cracked nutshells were still in the trash. Carefully, Bigalow dropped an unbroken half-shell onto the floor beside the trash basket. It rocked back and forth like a tiny boat. To make sure of the fit, Bigalow hopped down and sat in it. It was perfect!

Getting the thread and the shell up the stairs to T.J.'s room was a long and difficult struggle. For one awful minute, the walnut shell slipped out of his tiny paws and fell all the way back down to the bottom of the stairs. At that point, Bigalow burst into tears.

As weary as he was, the little mouse dried his tears and began again. He fought and struggled even harder than before, and finally, the shell and thread were pulled into T.J.'s room.

Bigalow left the walnut shell on the floor by the bedpost and climbed up to the balloon with the thread. For a long time, Bigalow chewed, knotted, and tied. When he was satisfied that every piece of thread was in just the right place, he dashed down to get the walnut shell. With a little more chewing, knotting, and tying, the shell was fastened to the dangling threads. It hung below the balloon like a tiny basket. When it was finished, Bigalow sat back on the bedpost, tired but happy. The big red balloon that shone so beautifully in the afternoon sun held the promise of great adventure!

Once more the little mouse raced down the stairs.
Soon it will be dark, he thought. There wasn't much time!
Quickly he collected cheese bits and bread scraps from
the trash.

In a flash, he wrapped his little "picnic" into a bundle
and raced back to the waiting balloon. He must leave
right away. They could come any minute! If that
happened he would lose the beautiful red balloon *and*
his adventure!

Up the bedpost he ran. Quickly, he chewed through the string tied to the bedpost and leaped headfirst into the waiting walnut shell. Slowly . . . ever so s-l-o-w-l-y, the balloon began to rise. In a moment, it was caught by the soft afternoon breeze. Gently, it whirled over the bed.

Suddenly, the balloon rose higher and gathered speed.

Just then, Bigalow heard Granny's car rumbling into the driveway.

The balloon dipped dangerously low over T.J.'s dresser. Bigalow was terrified. He held his breath as tears of fear sprang to his eyes. Inches from a terrible crash into the lamp, the balloon lifted once more. At last—at last . . . it found its way to the open window.

Below him, Bigalow heard T.J. and Katie shouting.

They must see the balloon in the window! he thought frantically.

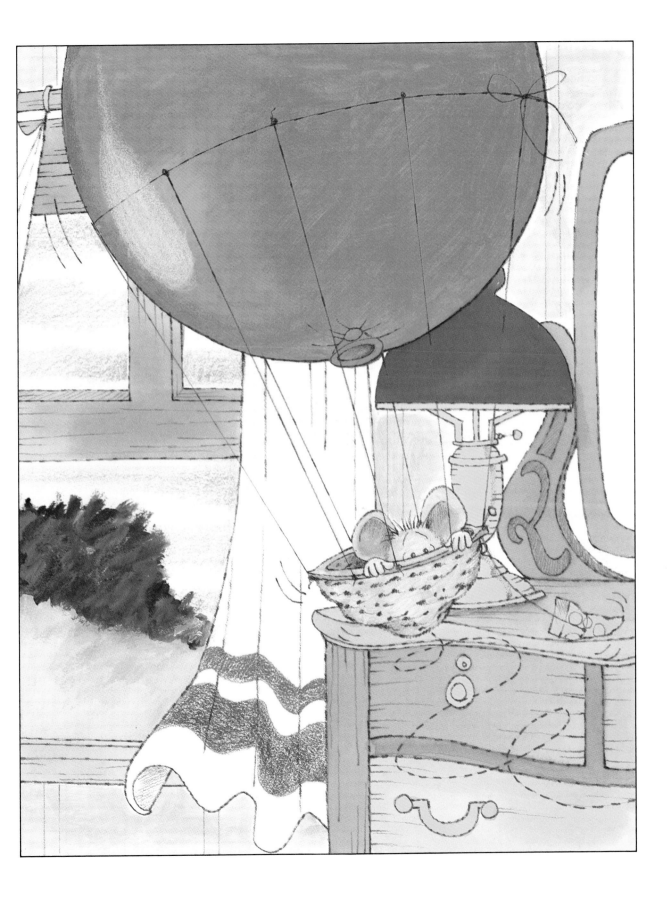

For one horrible minute, the balloon stuck! Scrape . . . scrape . . . sccraaape . . *puk*!

T.J. and Katie burst breathlessly into the room just as the beautiful red balloon finally broke free on a gust of cool evening air.

"I'm out! I am really, really out!" squeaked Bigalow joyfully.

As the wonderful red balloon took Bigalow higher and higher, T.J.'s and Katie's voices became fainter and Granny's house grew smaller and smaller, finally disappearing from view.

The streaks of a pink-red sunset were filling the evening sky now. Soon the moon would rise. From a tree far below, a bird whispered the day's last song. In the walnut shell under that big red balloon, a little mouse's heart pounded with excitement as he thought to himself. . . . *This is only the beginning!*

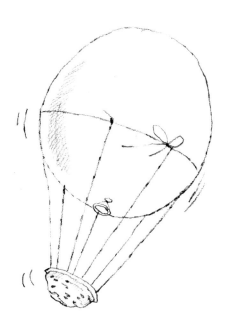

But it was still morning for T.J. and Katie.

"That was the best make-believing we've ever done!" said T.J.

"I really felt like I *was* Bigalow," said Katie.

Granny Rose's old car was coming to a stop by a large emerald lake surrounded by big shady trees and picnic tables.

"This is it—we're here!" Granny announced.

"Already!" Katie sat up and looked around.

"Time goes so fast when we make-believe," said T.J.

"It sure does," agreed Katie hopping from the car.

As they ran toward the lake, Katie grabbed T.J.'s hand and looked up. "Keep watching, T.J. We could see a big red balloon today . . . a special 'Bigalow' balloon!"

Katie

"4"   "5"   "6" and the Grey one

cassandra